The Wide Open

**Jeffery Martin
Botzenhart**

ALL RIGHTS RESERVED

Publisher's Note:

This is a work of fiction. All names,
characters, places, and events are the work
of the author's imagination.

Any resemblance to real persons, places, or
events is coincidental.

Solstice Publishing -
www.solsticepublishing.com

The Wide Open

Jeffery Martin Botzenhart

To small town America,
never lose your innocence

Chapter One

Distracted by the tall, windblown prairie grass, Mason appreciated how the late afternoon sky was turning from blue to orange. This time of day, as well as the dawn, was his favorite, the colors breathtaking and beautiful.

He glanced down and returned to his task. "I brought Grandma with me today like I promised I would. I'm sorry I forgot to bring her the last time I was here." Digging his hands in the dirt next to his grandpa's low marble grave marker, he lowered his grandma's framed picture into the hole he'd made earlier. He covered it up with the loose dirt and placed several wild daisies on top. "Now you two can be together again."

Mason stood up and looked around the lonely graveyard surrounded by a dilapidated white picket fence. The dozen or so grave markers were well tended to by the loving hands of the Fulton Christian Women's Auxiliary. They were the sweetest five old ladies he knew. Each Saturday, rain, shine, or snow, they would drive out of town to come and tend to the graves. They were always asking the church congregation for volunteers. Mason was one of the few to come when needed.

He regretted that his grandma's grave was far away in Bismarck. She had died twenty-one years ago, before he was born. Every day his grandpa showed his devotion for her simply by talking to thin air, imagining her standing by his side. Each night he would tell her he loved her, and how wonderful it would be when they were together again in Heaven.

That memory brought up another of Mason's regrets, that his grandpa was buried here and not next to her in Bismarck. The last fifteen or so years had been hard, money-wise, and the expense to bury him next to her cost too much. All Mason could afford was this simple plot out here amidst the wide open of North Dakota. He worried his grandpa would be disappointed in him because of this, but there was nothing else he could do.

Sighing, he thought, *I miss you. I wish you were still here.* A stray gust of wind brushed his cheek, bringing a smile. The last night his grandpa was alive he told Mason that when he felt the wind suddenly caress his skin, he would be there with him. *Now I miss you more.*

Riding his old ten-speed bicycle away from the cemetery, he steered it further into an area of the wide open unspoiled by trees. The vast expanse ahead of fields of plush waving grass reflected the low-hanging sun in a deeper orange sky. If someone desired a place of serenity, this is where they would find it.

When Mason reached the intersection of two dirt roads, he found his friend, Jared, waiting there for him. Stamping out his cigarette, Jared smiled and waved as Mason stopped his bicycle.

"I hope you weren't waiting too long."

Shaking his head, Jared replied, "I'm not in any hurry to go home. Here, a soda for you and a beer for me."

Mason took the glass bottle from Jared and the two silently toasted. They were exact opposites, his friend shorter than him with long hair, and a beard. Jared always kidded Mason about his tall, handsome, boy-next-door good looks.

"What time does the bus pick you up at the edge of town?"

"Around ten." Kicking at the dirt, Jared added, "You *know*…I bet there's room for one more on that bus. You and I could leave this small town together, never look back."

Mason looked down at his worn sneakers and responded, "No. I'm sorry… but this is where I belong."

"Why? What's keeping you here? Your grandpa died a month ago, leaving you with a run-down silver rust bucket of a camping trailer to call home. You don't have enough money to keep gas in that old pickup truck of his or even put decent food on the table."

"I'm doing fine," Mason insisted, hiding his concern over this.

"But you could be doing so much better," Jared argued. "Your carpentry skills alone could get you a top paying job, not to mention you're the smartest twenty-year-old man I know…except when it comes to this town. Trust me, this isn't everyone's idea of the American Dream."

"Maybe the wide open isn't meant for you, but as I said, this is where I belong."

"You're right, this isn't where I want to be. We both know why you won't admit this to yourself."

Mason shifted his weight uncomfortably, knowing what Jared was thinking.

"They aren't coming back, your dad and mom. Twelve years ago, they left you with your grandpa. If they were coming back for you, they would have done so a long time ago."

The truth in Jared's comment opened old wounds that had never healed. Feeling the sting of tears in his eyes, Mason hid this by turning away and staring out at the brilliant orange sun setting in the distance. Swallowing hard, he wanted to say something, tell Jared off, but deep down he knew his friend might be right. His parents weren't coming back.

"I'm sorry. I had no right to say that," Jared apologized. "It's just that... I don't know what I'm going to do without you. You've been my best friend for as long as I can remember. I wouldn't have survived all these years without you. Either in a few minutes or a few hours that all comes to an end."

"It doesn't have to. Maybe someday you'll come back here."

"No, there's no coming back for me."

Uncomfortable with his thoughts about not seeing his friend again, Mason wondered, "So where are you heading?"

"My dad thinks the army recruiters are meeting me tomorrow morning in Bismarck. By the time he finds out I lied to him, I'll be in California making a new life for myself. I sold my cell phone...so he won't be able to call or locate me. I paid cash for an airplane ticket to Los Angeles. From there I'm going to disappear, see what's waiting for me."

"I wish things were different between you two."

"Every time he beat me... I wished the same." Jared sounded angry after admitting this,

Forcing a smile on his face, he hugged Mason, even messing his short dark hair. "Come home with me," he urged. "You can have some barbecue chicken and a beer, not a soda."

Mason grinned, "You know I only drink milk and soda... and I'm the last person your dad would want in his house. I'm white trash."

"You aren't white trash."

"That's what your dad called me more than once."

"Well in a few hours he's not going to be my dad anymore. Come on, let's go torture him. You know you want to."

"I can't. I have to be at work in about an hour. I gotta get going."

"So this is it," Jared said, looking away from Mason.

"Yeah, I guess so."

Again Jared hugged him, this time tighter, not seeming to want to let go.

"Don't get lost out here in the wide open," he warned.

"I'll be here if you ever decide to come back."

"I know you will."

Mason rode off, looking back once to see Jared still standing there watching him leave. Picking up his speed, when the sun was halfway down, he reached the edge of town. He pulled off the road and parked his bicycle next to an old vacant gas station his dad used to bring him to before they left.

He walked up to the dust-encrusted windows and tried to look inside. All he could see was a whole lot of nothing. But anything inside wasn't why he stopped. What caught his attention was a vintage, red, white, and blue soda vending machine. The last thing his dad bought him was a bottle of soda from this machine. Most people probably thought of it as a piece of junk. For Mason, it represented the last moment he bonded with his dad. He never saw him again after this. Wanting the machine to look a little less lonely, with his finger he drew a smiley face in the dust covering the glass front. He'd hoped it would make him feel better, but it didn't.

***

Opening the roadside motel room door, Scarlett was surprised by what she found. She expected it to be cold and sterile like so many other motel rooms she'd stayed in. This place was different. A wrought-iron bed covered with a colorful patchwork quilt reminded her of her bedroom back home in Fargo. White lace linen curtains, an antique-looking dresser, and twin chairs flanking a small fireplace enhanced the homey impression of the room. It lacked the modern conveniences of a refrigerator and television but did have a bathroom and an old telephone.

"This is real nice," Clint, her boyfriend commented as he brought in her suitcase and a six-pack of beer. "All that's left to bring in is the diaper bag," he added as he stepped outside.

Cradling their one-month-old son, Kyle, in her arms, She glanced down, seeing how peaceful his sleep appeared. She stepped further into the room, admiring a painting hung above the bed, featuring running wild horses. She hoped Kyle would grow up in a room like this in their forever home someday. But forever wasn't on the horizon, or at least she couldn't tell if it was.

Clint dropped the diaper bag near the door and kissed her cheek as he quickly headed for the bathroom. Leaving the door wide open, while peeing he called to her, "I'm glad I spotted this place before we drove out of town. It might have been hours before we found another motel."

Scarlett was glad too but would have been much happier had it been just her and Kyle. At one time she would have been okay to have Clint there with them, yet her feelings for him had changed months ago. He had never been, nor ever would be the man of her dreams, though maybe he thought so. She didn't love him but for now, was all she had. Clint was the first guy to take an interest in her. Her parents hated him, thinking he was a freeloader and would never amount to anything. They were right. In the end, her strained relationship with her parents drew her to him. And one night of unprotected sex ended with her getting pregnant.

Clint walked up behind her and held her in his arms. "I have an idea," he said. "You and Kyle have been together every minute since he was born. Why don't you put on something nice and go downtown, get out for a little while. At the far end of the street was that little restaurant. Go get yourself a piece of pie and some ice cream on top," he suggested. "I'll stay here with

Kyle. He'll probably sleep the whole time you're gone."

"I don't know," Scarlett responded, concerned about leaving Kyle with Clint. He hadn't shown any real paternal instinct for their son. She couldn't remember him holding Kyle more than once.

"Go on. Kyle needs some alone time with his daddy."

That's the first time I think he's referred to himself as his daddy, she thought. Hearing this made her smile. Maybe she was worrying over nothing.

"Go on," he again urged. "I'll spread a blanket on the floor and surround it with pillows. He's too small to hardly move any. We'll be fine."

"Well… okay… I guess." Her heart still wasn't comfortable leaving Kyle, but Clint was right. She could use a little alone time. Opening her suitcase, she found some clothes to change into. Putting on a white dress with thin straps, she then fussed with her shoulder-length brown hair. Adding white sneakers and gold-hooped earrings to her outfit, for the first time in months she thought, *I look pretty.*

"Wow," Clint complimented her when she came out of the bathroom. "I'm one lucky guy to be with such a beautiful woman."

"Thanks," she said, feeling a little self-conscious as she brushed strands of hair away from her eyes.

"Don't rush back. We'll be just fine. This seems like a nice small town, a great place to explore on a Friday night."

"Okay."

Again he kissed her cheek. She smiled and looked over at Kyle, asleep on a blanket just like Clint said he would be. She wanted to lay down and cuddle with him, but Clint needed this time with him. She figured she'd be gone less than an hour, or maybe just a half-hour at most.

Chapter Two

Clint's comment about downtown proved an exaggeration. Only a main street and a few side buildings made up Fulton, North Dakota. That didn't bother Scarlett in the least. The town had a charm about it that she found appealing. The mostly brick buildings, probably constructed in the fifties or before were well maintained. Though there was only one traffic light, at the only intersection, antique street lamps lined the sidewalks. Since it was after eight in the evening, all the stores were closed. *That must be what it's like out here*, she thought. *Actually, it's kind of nice. I like the quiet.*

Being June, and with the longest day of the year on Sunday, the evening air retained the sun's warmth. Glancing toward the end of the street, she saw that two fireflies had already begun signaling to each other. She looked back at the western molasses-colored sky and setting orange sun, thinking about summer evenings at home with her parents. Gliding on the porch swing, waiting for the dark starlit sky to appear was a memory she held dear to her.

Walking by a thrift store, a general store, a post office, and a beauty salon, she saw two men enter what she guessed was a bar on the street corner. Having never consumed alcohol, she steered clear of this, heading instead for the restaurant still open.

After stepping inside, Scarlett found the place mostly empty of customers. "What's your pleasure, honey?" a waitress asked from behind the counter.

Seeing an apple pie in the display case, Scarlett answered, "A piece of pie, please."

"Would you like a scoop of ice cream on that?"

"Yes, please."

"Coming right up."

Scarlett sat on a stool at the counter and looked around. About a dozen booths lined the wall of windows, and an old jukebox sat between the restroom doors. *I bet this place has been around for a long time. It would be nice to come here every now and then.*

The waitress set her pie and ice cream down, drawing her away from her thoughts.

"Where is everyone?" Scarlett asked. "I guess I thought there would be more people here tonight."

"It was busy earlier," the waitress answered. "But it's a nice Friday night. Everyone will be heading to the drive-in movie theater just up the road past the church. That's what folks here do on a Friday night, from late spring to mid-fall."

"Is there a good movie playing tonight?"

"They only show older family type movies. I think tonight is *Willy Wonka and the Chocolate Factory*. The kids love that one, adults too."

"Sounds nice."

"You should go check it out."

"Maybe I will… for a little while."

After Scarlett paid for and ate her pie, she left the restaurant and walked up the road to her right. A wide open field glittered with the lights of countless fireflies. Further up, on the lawn in front of a white steepled church, she saw a help wanted sign, advertising for a part-time receptionist. *I'd apply for that job if we weren't heading for Denver. It would be great to stay here and raise Kyle in a small town like this.* Thinking about her son, she thought, *I should get back to him and Clint*. It had only been a half-hour, though. *I'll only stay at the drive-in for a few minutes, just to see what it's like.*

Walking down the road, passing by another field, she spotted the lights of the drive-in movie theater sign. She grinned at the retro neon-lit rocket and the words, *Skyway Drive-In*. There were older cars parked, and she saw people heading for the concession stand. She guessed the movie would be starting soon.

An old couple, sitting in lawn chairs, were taking money to enter.

"How much is it to get in?" Scarlett asked the woman.

Adjusting her nineteen-sixties style glasses on the bridge of her nose, the old woman smiled and answered, "Five dollars per car…but since you walked, it'll only be a dollar."

"That's not expensive at all," Scarlett commented as she paid.

"We don't run this for the money," the woman answered. "It's just nice for everyone to get together. Times being what they are, too many are missing the simple pleasures of life."

I like her answer and her.

"Now, make sure you stop at the stand over there and get a treat." Leaning forward and covering her mouth with her hand, clearly not wanting the man to hear, the woman whispered, "They boy running it a handsome treat, himself."

"I'll keep that in mind."

Kids running here and there and parents talking to each other was pleasant to see. To her, it seemed that she had traveled back to a more innocent point in time, when the American dream was alive and well.

Over her shoulder, she heard a deep voice ask, "What could I get you?"

Turning, she quickly understood what the old woman meant. The young man behind the counter might be the handsomest she'd ever seen. His short dark hair, blue eyes, and dimpled-smile were dreamy. The white T-shirt he wore looked like it had been painted on his muscular frame. For the first time since she could recall, butterflies surged inside her.

"Is there something I could get you?" he again asked.

Your name would be nice, she thought. Composing herself, she looked at the menu and answered, "I'd like a cherry soda."

He reached into a cooler and pulled out a glass bottle, handing it to her. "One cherry soda."

"How much do I owe you?"

"Just a smile. Everything is free," he responded.

"Thank you," Scarlett said and shyly grinned.

"You're welcome."

When she turned to leave he said, "My name is Mason."

"I'm Scarlett."

"That's a pretty name."

"Thanks." She wasn't sure if it was the night heat or a blush warming her skin. She stepped over to a picnic table and sat down. When the movie started, she glanced over and saw him looking at her. She returned his smile and wave, smitten by his attention.

***

"Leaving so soon?" Mason asked as she was heading for the exit.

"I have to get back," she responded.

"You're not from around here."

"No, I'm just passing through."

He smiled at her. She could tell, though, that there was some disappointment he hid.

"If I'm not being too forward, I could walk you back to where you're staying," Mason offered.

"No, that's all right. I'll be fine." Now she was feeling the disappointment too.

"Maybe next time you pass through you might want to come to another movie."

"I'd like that. Good night."

"Good night."

The whole way back to the motel all Scarlett could think about was Mason. His blue eyes, good looks, and smile had charmed her like never before. Clint, a little shorter and on the heavy side, was no comparison to Mason. She knew she had just met the boy next door, the one always talked about, a girl's American dream.

Approaching the motel, she immediately went into panic mode when she found Clint's black Mustang missing. *What's going on?* She rushed up to the door, finding it unlocked. Feeling her heart choking her throat, her trembling hand could barely push the door in. A lamp on one of the nightstands dimly lit the room. Her suitcase, the car seat, and the diaper bag were still there.

Holding her breath, feeling light-headed as if she were about to pass out, Scarlett stepped passed the bed and felt relief flood over her. Kyle was still sleeping on his blanket.

She sat on the edge of the bed and gripped the headboard to steady herself. Glancing around, all traces of Clint were gone except the six-pack of beer he had brought in. She remembered him carrying his suitcase in first, but it wasn't here now.

It didn't take more than a few seconds to realize, *the son-of-a-bitch left me again.*

He had done this before after finding out she was pregnant. A month before she gave birth he came back, begging her forgiveness. He claimed he was scared. She was too. Somehow he convinced her to take him back, that everything would be great this time. *How could I have been so stupid? Why did I believe you?*

Wanting to cry, she looked around the motel room and whispered, "Now what?" She knew she had less than twenty dollars in her purse, not enough for bus tickets back home to Fargo. That wasn't where she wanted to go. Neither was Denver, Clint's dream.

She noticed a piece of paper on the nightstand and picked it up. It was the receipt for the room. At first, she was confused to see that Clint had paid for the whole weekend, not just one night. This confirmed her suspicions further that his intention had been to leave her and their son all long.

As she kept thinking about him, her anger grew. Seeing the beer again, she stood up and grabbed the six-pack. She took it into the bathroom and walked over to the sink. Opening the first can, she intended to pour it down the drain. Too many times she'd seen smart people become dumb when drinking beer. She asked her mom once why people liked it. The answer she got was that some didn't. They just drank it to numb their thoughts and forget about their troubles. Right about now that sounded pretty good. So instead of pouring it down the drain, she took a sip. Though it tasted worse than anything she drank before, she took another sip and another.

Chapter Three

"This is just what I needed," Mason sarcastically mumbled when he found his bicycle in the dumpster behind the concession building. Dragging it out, he discovered his back tire flat. It didn't really upset him since this wasn't the first time it happened. *It's sad that I'm used to this…but tonight is warm, and home is only a few miles away. I guess while walking tonight I can look at the stars on my way home.*

He'd kept himself busy at the concession stand these last few hours, drawing away thoughts of Jared leaving. When he wasn't working at the drive-in or doing odd jobs around town and Jared wasn't laboring on his parent's farm, they were always together. Other than fishing at their favorite pond or playing baseball with the church team, the rest of the time they spent walking around or driving through the countryside. *The wide open's gonna be a bit lonelier,* he thought.

A hushed, gentle breeze passed through tall grasses on both sides of the road. Someone once told him the ocean made the same sound at night. During the summer, he kept the windows open and imagined he was at the beach with his parents. He remembered his mom promising him they would go there someday. *Did you and Dad ever make it there? Was it just like you said it would be?*

The subtle tingling of wind chimes alerted him to a dark house as he walked by. Reaching the mailbox, he heard a sultry voice say, "Hey there, handyman. I got something that needs fixin'."

He tried to hide his nerves when the sheriff's wife approached him. Wearing only her silky slip and holding a bottle of wine and a glass, she padded barefoot around him. Touching his arms and chest as if he was an object she was thinking of buying, she took a sip from her glass and teased, "Cat got your tongue?"

"What do you need me to fix?" he finally asked and silently guessed her answer.

"It's my body. It hasn't been used for a while," she answered, pressing her glass to her breasts.

I don't want my first time to be with the drunken wife of the sheriff, he silently said to himself.

"I'm sure your husband wouldn't like you saying this to me," he warned.

"He won't care. He's not even here. It's just you and me."

"Where is he?"

"Some drunk drove his Mustang into a utility pole. He died in the crash. My husband will be gone for hours cleaning up that mess."

"I should be going," Mason said, hoping to end this conversation.

"You're just like him, running away when a woman wants to talk."

"I think your husband would be the better man to talk to."

"I would think that *too*...but here I am...*alone*. No, not alone. We're here, the two of us. Want some of this cheap wine?"

"No, Ma'am."

"You know, I wanted you the first time I saw you," she confessed. "You were mowing the church lawn. You had your shirt off, exposing those impressive sun-bronzed muscles of yours. Why, for a lonely woman like me, seeing that caused me some very inappropriate notions. I can hardly control myself when I see you. Tonight...I don't want to control myself."

Even more uncomfortable with what she was saying, he again tried to leave, but she stopped him.

"What is it with this town, this place? When I first met Tom... he was a different man, fun, spontaneous, passionate. When we left Kansas City and came here, all that changed. It's like this place made him drowsy. I can't even recognize the man I fell in love with. It felt like stepping out of the sunlight into the darkest room. I wasn't prepared for all this darkness."

"Sheriff Crawford seems like a good man," Mason responded in his defense.

"He is a good man," she agreed. "He just isn't the man I want anymore. I want the one I met in Kansas City. Tom doesn't see how much he's changed, or how much I have. All this wide open space has made him blind. He thinks we're happy and I pretend we are. He even wants a baby…but I take a little pill to spoil that dream. If I had his child out here, that would be a death sentence for me. He'd never want to leave."

"Have you asked him to?"

"Not directly. I've hinted a few times about wanting to return to Kansas City."

"Why not tell him how you feel? Why pretend you're happy when you're not?"

"Because I know he doesn't want to leave."

"Do you love your husband?"

She hesitated before answering, "No, not anymore."

"Then why stay if he and this place make you so miserable?"

"Maybe I'm just afraid of being alone. I know how strange that sounds. I'm lonely but afraid of being by myself. I'm forty years old. How do I start over...and who would even want me? Clearly, you don't."

"I'm sorry you're so unhappy," Mason offered.

"So am I." Stepping closer to him, she added, "But you can make me less lonely tonight. Come on, lie to me for an hour. And, if you can't lie, pretend you're someone else. I do it all the time."

"No, I can't.

"Of course you can't," she laughingly agreed. "Like I said, you're just like him."

"Good night, Mrs. Crawford."

"Good night, handyman."

***

Guessing where the accident might be, as well as Sheriff Crawford, Mason turned around and headed back to town. *What will it be like the next time I see him and his wife? I'll probably see them both tomorrow and at church on Sunday. How am I ever going to look at them the same knowing what I know now?*

Mason saw the traffic light turn red. There were no cars waiting to go when the light turned green again. For such a small town as Fulton, he wondered why it was even needed. Maybe this was a part of small-town life. Do all small towns have one? He thought *no*.

Except for the sound of a dog barking close by, downtown Fulton appeared as abandoned as the old gas station on the edge of town. The darkened store windows and dim streetlamps didn't make it scary at all, just lonely. *Maybe this is what Mrs. Crawford was talking about?* He knew for himself how in quiet places like this you could clearly hear your own thoughts. Maybe her's were too loud.

As he began walking by the roadside motel, he saw Scarlett, the pretty girl he'd talked to at the drive in. But she wasn't acting like she did earlier. Seeing her stumble and then fall to her knees, he rushed over and asked, "Are you okay?"

Scarlett looked up at him, her eyes drowsy and not seeming in focus. When she tried speaking, her words were slurred. He didn't understand any of what she said.

She pointed to the open door at the end of the motel. "That must be your room," he said. "Come on. Let me help you inside."

Mason leaned his bicycle against the outside wall of the motel and then helped Scarlett stand. She teetered as he held on to her. The stench of beer on her breath revealed why she was acting this way. After taking an unsteady step with her, he stopped. "I'm gonna have to carry you inside. I hope you don't mind." She offered no protests as he picked her up. Resting her head against his chest, she stopped talking. He glanced down and saw that she'd passed out. He was relieved that her breathing seemed okay.

Flicking a light switch just inside the door, the lamp on the nightstand closest to them turned on. He carried her to the bed and gently laid her down. He brushed her long hair away from her face and covered her with an extra blanket even though it wasn't cold in the room.

He turned off the light and was about to leave when he heard a soft sound coming from the far side of the room. On the floor there, he found a baby who was beginning to fuss. *This little one can't be more than a month or two old*, he guessed.

"Well, what do we have here?" Mason whispered as he knelt. The baby started crying. "Hey, there. Why the tears?"

Picking the baby up, he cradled the baby in his arms, rocking just a little. "So what's the trouble here? Maybe you're hungry? Is that it?" Feeling the diaper, he knew that could use a change.

Scarlett wasn't going to wake anytime soon, so he turned on the lamp near where he found the baby and spotted the diaper bag. With one hand, he rummaged through it, finding a diaper, a bottle, and some powdered formula. "It's your lucky day," he whispered. "A fresh diaper and a midnight snack coming up."

Changing the wet diaper, he softly said, "Since I don't know your name, little guy, I'm just gonna call you *pal*. I hope that's all right. My name is Mason. It's a pleasure to meet you." He looked over at Scarlett and then back to the baby. "Listen up, pal, I don't think your mom is feeling too good about now. I don't feel right leaving you alone with her if she's going to be sick. And yeah, she's gonna be sick. So if you don't mind, how about I stay with you until she's feeling better? What do you say?"

Mason tenderly ran his fingers through the baby's feathery brown hair. He seemed to like this. After feeding him a bottle, then he burped him. The baby spit up a little on his T-shirt. "Don't you worry about that. It smelled like hot dogs and caramel corn and was headed for the wash. I probably stink real bad."

Placing the baby down on the blanket, Mason took off his shirt and tossed it over by the door. He again picked up the baby and held him close. Resting his head against Mason's chest, the baby found a comfortable spot, growing calm almost instantly. Mason smiled as his tiny fingers rubbed the hair on his chest while he walked him around the room.

The baby fell asleep within minutes. Mason gently returned him to the blanket spread on the floor and covered him with another blanket. He then took the extra pillow off the bed. Kicking off his shoes, he laid next to the baby and watched him. *I wonder if my mom and dad ever did this with me? Neither ever said so. I don't remember a whole lot about them anymore, just a few memories.*

Scarlett's snoring put him at ease, and helped reduce his worrying about her. *You're going to have one bad headache in the morning. I wonder why you decided to get drunk? When we met tonight at the drive-in, I never would have guessed this. What made you do it?*

Other things crossed his mind too as he watched the baby sleep. *How did you both even get here? I didn't see a car or truck parked outside. The bus doesn't come into town. You have to go all the way over to the highway and wait for it to stop. That's about three miles away. Did you walk here?*

Mason rolled onto his back and looked up at the dark ceiling. He blinked a few times as his eyes grew too heavy to stay open. Being a light sleeper, he knew he'd wake up if the baby fussed again. "Good night, Scarlett," he whispered. "I hope you won't be mad I stayed here tonight. I'll explain everything in the morning. Sweet dreams."

Chapter Four

At first, when Scarlett opened her eyes, everything was blurry. *Where am I?* she thought. She couldn't remember suffering such an awful taste in her mouth or the severe throbbing pain in her head. Her stomach felt queasy, but she didn't think she needed to throw up, at least not yet.

Rolling onto her back, she brushed the hair away from her eyes as she looked at the ceiling. *What happened? Why do I feel like this?* A minute later, the answer to both questions came to her. *I got drunk.*

She sat up and waited for the room to stop spinning before attempting to stand. After staggering over to the bathroom door, she kicked something as she walked over to the sink. Glancing down, she found beer cans littering the floor. She couldn't remember if she drank all six but really didn't care how many there were. One was too many in her now educated opinion for beer drinking.

Turning on the faucet, the sound of running water hurt her ears. Capturing some in her open palms, she splashed her face twice. Growing more alert, she dried her cheeks and looked at her reflection in the mirror. "I am never doing that again," she vowed.

Returning to the bed, she tripped over a blanket left on the floor. "Dear God," she uttered. Covering her mouth with her hands, she stifled her panicked shrill at finding Kyle missing. Searching the room, she trembled with fear. Her son was gone.

Scarlett rushed to the door, letting it fly open as she bolted outside. What she saw not only stopped her but also left her speechless. There, wandering around barefoot and bare chested was the young man she met at the drive-in. She remembered his name, Mason. In his arms, he was cradling Kyle who seemed completely at peace.

"Do you see that sky out there?" Mason quietly asked Kyle. "There's an old saying, something about red skies in the morning and at night. That red color out there is a warning that it's going to rain. But don't you worry. Your mom's gonna keep you safe."

What struck Scarlett most was how natural this looked to her as if her son was always meant to be held by this young man. His ear was resting on Mason's chest and his tiny fingers were scratching the hair on his skin. A notion crossed her mind about Mason. *I could easily fall in love with you. I think Kyle already has.*

"Look over there, pal. Your mom's awake."

Mason walked over to her but she stepped back from taking her son and shook her head. "You keep holding him," she said. "He's comfortable in your arms."

"I should explain," Mason offered.

"Me too," she responded.

Mason went first. "Well…when I was walking home last night I found you outside, stumbling around. You were…"

"Drunk," Scarlett interrupted.

"Yeah. Anyway, I carried you inside and was about to leave when I heard this little guy fussing."

"His name is Kyle."

"That's a good name for a boy."

She smiled, remembering that Clint hated the name.

"I knew you weren't going to be feeling well, so I stayed to take care of him while you slept. I took real good care of him. I promise. I changed his diaper and fed him a bottle. He spit up a little on my shirt, but it was dirty anyway."

"I know you took good care of him," Scarlett agreed. "Just look at how calm he is in your arms. It's like he's always belonged there."

"He's a nice little boy."

"I think you'll be a good daddy someday."

Mason grinned. "I hope to be."

"Thank you for being so kind to both of us."

Mason smiled and nodded his head.

"So now it's my turn to explain what happened. I want you to know. I'm a good mother. I…"

"I know you are," Mason stopped her. "Just by how you rushed out of the room searching for him, I knew then. Just by the way you look at him, I can tell. It's how a mom should look at her baby."

"I didn't leave him alone last night when I met you at the drive-in. When I left him, he was with his daddy. No, he was with his biological father. Clint was never his daddy. Deep down I knew he didn't want to be."

"So… where is Clint?"

"I don't know. When I came back to the motel room, he was gone. He took all his stuff and left."

"Why would he do that to you and Kyle?"

"It wasn't the first time he left me. When I was pregnant, he took off for a few months. But he came back, all sorry for leaving me. He said things would be different this time. I guess I wanted to believe it."

"I'm sorry."

Running her hands through her hair, Scarlett blurted, "I'm not. I was angry…which resulted in me getting drunk. But truth be told, I'm not sorry he's gone. I didn't love him…and I'm pretty sure he didn't love me."

"So, now what?"

"Well…I have today and tomorrow to decide that. The room is paid for through the weekend. Come Monday morning, I need to figure out what's next for Kyle and me."

"Do you have any family close by?"

"My parents live across state, over in Fargo. I'm not sure they want to hear from me."

"Why?"

"Because… they consider themselves upstanding Christians who were disappointed their nineteen-year-old daughter got pregnant out of wedlock. My father insisted I give Kyle up for adoption, but I just couldn't. They asked me to leave when I refused. I'm not sure they will even talk to me now."

"Is there anyone else?"

"No one I can think of. Listen, this isn't your problem. I don't regret getting pregnant and keeping Kyle. I'll figure something out. Here, let me take him from you."

"I… could watch him a little while longer if you wanted to change or something like that."

Scarlett could tell that Mason wanted to hold him more. "Thanks. I could use a long shower to get rid of yesterday."

"Take all the time you need. He's in good hands."

"I know he is."

Mason stopped her from going inside by asking, "Would you and Kyle like to go to a church social? Tomorrow is the Summer Solstice, the longest day of the year. Starting at noon, the church has all kinds of things to do until sundown. It's a real nice time."

Judging from his expression, she knew he wanted her to say yes. It's what she wanted too. "That sounds wonderful. We'd love to go."

Mason beamed with her answer until he blushed when she asked, "Should we consider this a date?"

"I… don't know. I mean… if you want to."

"Yeah, I want to."

"Okay then."

***

All Mason could think about while walking home was Scarlett and Kyle. Even after a rough night, she was as pretty as the first moment he saw her. And her son awakened something bittersweet inside him. *Did my dad ever hold me like I held Kyle? I wish my dad was here to answer that question.*

Hearing the sound of kids, he looked toward a large white farmhouse to his right. Frank and Deanna Shannon and their three sons lived there. The boys liked him, always asking him to play baseball when he was home. Not having grown up with many friends, Mason enjoyed being with them. The Shannon family never made him feel like some other people in town, people who looked down on him for being poor.

As the road crested on a slight incline, Mason stopped dead in his tracks, staring at his front yard. Trash covered much of what he could see. But more surprising was watching Jared's dad cleaning up the mess under the watchful eyes of Sheriff Crawford. Leaning against his police cruiser, the sheriff stared at Mister Hiram who was clearly unhappy.

Approaching Sheriff Crawford, Mason asked, "What's going on? Why is all this garbage spread in my yard?"

Without looking at Mason, the sheriff answered, "It appears that Mister Hiram wanted to remind you of your place in the community. The penalty for littering is cleaning up the mess...and a two hundred-dollar fine."

"*Two hundred dollars!*" Jared's dad protested.

"I'm sorry, *three* hundred. Care to make it four hundred?" Sheriff Crawford asked. Mister Hiram resumed cleaning up the mess while mumbling under his breath.

"Why are you so mean to me? What did I ever do to you?" Mason asked Jared's dad.

"Careful how you answer," Sheriff Crawford warned. Mister Hiram didn't respond.

When finished cleaning every piece of garbage off the grass, Mister Hiram loaded the bags into the bed of his pickup truck. He stepped over to Mason and the sheriff and finally offered, "We don't like your kind around here. Fulton is a safe little town. We don't want you following in your daddy's footsteps."

"What does that mean?"

"Oh, come on now. Don't play stupid. Everyone knows. By now, you must too."

"Now it's four hundred," Sheriff Crawford said. "The next mean thing you say will land you in jail. I would be very careful if I were you."

"I don't have that kind of cash on me," Jared's dad responded.

"Then write a check. Everyone knows you carry your checkbook with you." As Mister Hiram began writing the check, Sheriff Crawford added, "Be sure to make that out to Mason Keller." Jared's dad huffed but did as he was told. Once done, he tried handing the check to the sheriff. Sheriff Crawford pointed to Mason. Showing reluctance, Mister Hiram held out the check for Mason to take.

Holding it in his hands, Mason looked at the check as if it was something he'd never seen before. He then ripped it up and handed the pieces back to Jared's dad, who's jaw had dropped.

"I don't want your money. I just want to be left alone."

Mister Hiram stuffed the torn check into his pocket and got back in his truck. He slowly drove away under the watchful eyes of Sheriff Crawford.

Swallowing hard, and feeling unnerved standing there alone with the sheriff, Mason worried, *does he know his wife came on to me last night? Is that why he's here?*

Hoping it wasn't, and that he didn't know, instead, Mason asked, "What did he mean about my dad?"

"I don't make a habit of spreading gossip," Sheriff Crawford answered. "Let me know if he gives you any more trouble."

Before getting in his police cruiser, Mason halted him with another question. "How did you know he was over here doing this?"

The sheriff hesitated for a moment before responding, "I was just driving by…and I caught him."

I can't remember the last time you drove down this old dirt road. Were you really just driving by? Mason thought. *Or was there another reason?*

***

"Hi, Daddy. It's Scarlett."

Her stomach was in knots the whole time the operator placed the collect call to her parents. She wasn't sure either would accept the call, but her dad did. She could hear his shallow breaths. He didn't speak a word to her, adding to her misery.

"I guess you didn't expect to hear from me again. We didn't, I mean, well…things weren't right when I left. I know how angry and hurt you were with me. I don't blame you. A lot of things were said in anger." Nervous tremors shook her as she continued. "Um… a month ago… I had a baby boy. His name is Kyle. He's so small and sweet. He has my eyes."

Scarlett thought she heard her dad sniffle as if he was crying. Her heart broke, knowing this.

"Daddy, Clint… well, he left me again, I think for good this time. You were right about him. I just wanted—I don't know what I wanted. Anyway, he stranded Kyle and me in a small town called Fulton, on the other side of the state. I don't know what I'm gonna do. I want to come home, if that's all right. But I need you to understand that I'm not going to give Kyle up for adoption. *I'm* his mother. No one else is gonna raise him." After a long pause, Scarlett begged, "Daddy, please talk to me. Please say something." His response was silence.

Seeing Kyle squirming, she knew he'd want a bottle. *I guess this was pointless. The roads I've traveled don't lead home anymore.*

"Tell Momma I love her. I love you too. Bye, Daddy."

Just as she pulled the phone away from her ear, she heard her dad say, "Scarlett."

Chapter Five

After watching the sheriff drive away, leaving a cloud of dust behind him, Mason turned and looked at his grandpa's Airstream trailer. The polished silvery sheen had weathered away years ago, leaving a few spots of rust on the dulled exterior. He remembered being told stories of the places his grandparents traveled on vacation. From the Northern California coast to the barrier islands of Texas, he recalled everything his grandpa told him about those trips. Just a month after his grandma died, his grandpa put the trailer up on cement blocks, ending the miles of travel amidst the wide open of rural North Dakota.

He went inside and looked around, finding the kitchen and small living space spotless, something he'd learned from his grandpa. The appliances were old, but the metal and porcelain still held a polish to each. The floor was swept, and not one dirty dish was in sight. A place for everything and everything a place was the house rule. Having limited space, clutter could quickly pile up if not dealt with.

*I've been inside messy houses before
and walked through overgrown yards filled
with old tires and tossed away beer bottles,*
he thought. *No one, at least none that I
know of, called these people white trash like
they think of me. Why am I judged just
because of where I live? I learned to take
care of this place, to appreciate what I have.
Why do people want me to feel bad about
it? Who was it that came up with the idea
there's a right and wrong side of town?*

***

Before leaving yesterday, he'd left a box of
his grandpa's old photographs on the small
kitchen table. At first, he intended to return
them to his grandpa's dresser drawer, but he
wanted to relive the happier times, so he sat
down and opened the lid. His grandma's
picture lay on top. Grabbing a handful of
photographs, he started flipping through
them, and found moments captured on film
that represented each and every memory told
to him by his grandpa. Birthdays,
anniversaries, vacations, and a few random,
everyday moments made up his grandpa's
sacred collection.

As he reached the bottom of the box,
the next to last black-and-white photograph
confused him. Mason looked closer at the
picture of his grandparents standing in the

yard in front of the Shannons' large white farmhouse. *Why was this taken of them standing in front of the neighbor's house?* he wondered. *Grandpa said he only owned this trailer and the land under it.*

Mason stood up and walked over to the front window. Looking out toward his neighbors, their sons weren't outside, but Mister Shannon was. Needing to satisfy his curiosity, Mason headed over there to ask a few questions.

Crossing through a field of tall windswept grass, he noticed an odd color of blue in the sky, not fair weather-like but deeper, less vivid. *A storm's coming.*

Mason approached Mister Shannon, startling him with, "Good morning."

Mister Shannon, a tall, skinny, balding man in his mid-forties, turned around and smiled. It almost seemed forced. The Shannons had always been nice and welcoming. The forced smile had Mason feeling like a stranger standing there.

"Oh… good morning. What can I do for you?"

Mason noticed the tension in Mister Shannon's body language, how he uneasily shifted his weight. *I bet you're no good at telling a lie*, Mason guessed.

"I was wondering if you knew who owned your farm before you bought it."

Mister Shannon took a moment before he answered, "Well...I'm not sure. We've been here for five or six years. This farm was a foreclosure when we bought it from the bank. I don't think the previous owner's name was listed anywhere on the paperwork. Of course, there were a ton of papers to sign."

I got my answer. You're not a good liar.

"Why would you be wondering about that?" Mister Shannon asked.

Why are you hiding the answer to my question?

Mason held out the black-and-white photograph of his grandpa standing in front of the Shannons' house. Mister Shannon hesitated taking it, but did. Seeming mildly interested, he remarked, "Nice picture. Do you know when it was taken?"

"No. Until today I didn't know it existed. I was looking through some of my grandpa's old photographs when I found it. I was just curious why it was taken in front of your house."

"I'm sorry. I don't know," Mister Shannon responded, handing the photograph back to Mason. Sighing, he continued, "I've got some work to do on my truck. I'm sorry I couldn't answer your question." He turned away and resumed fixing something on the truck's engine.

You know something you're not telling me. Why? It's only a house.

Mason took a step back but stopped after seeing Mister Shannon's wife speaking to their sons on the porch. The boys kept looking at him as she quietly spoke. They seemed confused.

"Thanks, Mister Shannon. Oh…and…I promise not to come over anymore. I'm not sure what I did wrong, but whatever it was I'm sorry."

Mister Shannon stood up from being hunched over, keeping his back to Mason. He didn't say anything.

***

Mason rode his bicycle into town, parking it in front of Reddinger's General Store. A strong heated breeze created a wind tunnel through the buildings down the main street, tossing the traffic light like a kite in the wind. He looked up at the sky before heading inside. *A storm is coming. I hope it holds off until after tomorrow's church social.*

Peeling the straps of his backpack off his shoulders, Mason left it with his bicycle and bent down to tie his shoelaces. A nice, older couple, the Delaneys, stopped walking toward the store. Every week he cut their grass and did jobs around their house that Mister Delaney had trouble doing. Mason waved to them and was going to speak. They turned away before he could, clearly pretending not to notice him. At first, he wanted to approach them and ask why they were treating him like he didn't exist. But he guessed Jared's dad might have spread rumors around about him, leaving him wondering, *how many more people are going to treat me this way today?*

A bell hung on the door alerted Mister Reddinger that someone entered the store. Glancing up from the book he was reading, he saw Mason enter and tossed it aside. Mason couldn't help but notice how Mister Reddinger kept staring at him as if expecting him to do something wrong. *You've always been real nice to me, but not today. I feel like a prisoner being watched by a guard. So what crime did I commit?*

The floor space of the store was narrow, allowing only three aisles for merchandise. Miles away from the nearest department stores, Reddinger's was the only place to buy everyday items, from toothpaste and laundry soap to canned vegetables and dry cereal. Mister Reddinger made a trip every Monday to get more stuff to sell, gone from morning to night.

As he walked by one shelf to the next, he guessed Mister Reddinger was keeping a close eye on him. Testing his theory that he was being watched, Mason walked over to the farthest aisle away from the cash register. He grabbed a bottle of body wash off the shelf and wasn't surprised when he turned to see Mister Reddinger standing there, not too convincingly acting as if he was checking a price. Mason grabbed deodorant and a pack of chewing gum and stepped over to the register. Mister Reddinger stole a suspicious glance at him as he rang up the items.

"How is Mrs. Reddinger?" Mason asked.

"Fine." This one-word answer wasn't like him at all. Normally, if she wasn't around, he'd be complaining about her constant nagging, leading him to an early grave.

Frustrated to the point when he couldn't hold back, Mason blurted, "I didn't steal anything, if that's what you think. You know me. Check my pockets to make sure. I'll even strip down to my boxers." He swallowed hard as tears stung his eyes. "What did I do wrong. I have the right to know."

Mister Reddinger appeared unnerved by Mason's outburst, but held his tongue and handed Mason a plastic bag containing his purchases. For a split second, Mason thought he was going to answer him. He, instead, picked up his book and weakly nodded his head, dismissing Mason.

Returning to his bicycle, another man he knew, Ken Burke, stepped over to him. "Mason, you should probably go home."

"Why?" Mason quietly asked without making eye contact.

"You...just...should," Ken struggled to respond.

Mason stuffed the plastic bag into his backpack and quickly rode off.

***

At times, the gusting wind stirred up clouds of dust on the road ahead of him. Sweat drenched him from the sweltering heat, and the tears streamed down his cheeks as he rode up to the cemetery. The wood picket fence gate repeatedly banged as a shaft of sunlight pierced the gray clouds that looked like billowing plumes of smoke from a large fire.

Mason parked his bicycle and intended to seek out his grandpa's grave. Yet before he could, he spotted one of the old ladies who cared for the cemetery. She was sitting on the ground next to a headstone and was pulling weeds.

What if she won't talk to me either? Mason worried.

"Hello, Pauline," he hesitantly greeted.

"Hello, Mason," she offered. His anxiety eased when she spoke to him. "Not the nicest day, I'm afraid. They are calling for storms tomorrow for the church social," she commented. "I doubt we'll see much sunlight this weekend. Storms are coming. Mother Nature can show her bitchy side sometimes."

Mason knelt to her and remarked, "At least you're still talking to me."

The wide brim of her hat fluttered as she looked at him. "I've never been one who cared much for hateful gossip."

"What did I do to make everyone act strangely toward me? Please tell me."

Sighing, Pauline answered, "I don't think you've done anything to deserve the rotten treatment you're getting. Dearheart, it's not really about you, but more about your parents."

"My *parents*? What do they have to do with this?"

Pauline reached out, grasping Mason's hand. "What do you remember about them?"

"Not a whole lot. I mean, I remember my dad had tattoos on his arms and my mom was always laughing. There were times they were gone for weeks or even months at a time. Grandpa said they did missionary work."

"Hmm, I see," Pauline responded, not hiding her concern. "Is that what your grandpa told you?"

"Yeah."

She smiled. "I guess I understand why he did."

"Why he did what?"

"Why he kept the truth from you."

"What truth?"

Pauline looked away, struggling with what she wanted to say. Looking directly at him, she asked, "Do you trust that I wouldn't lie to you?"

"Yes, Ma'am."

"Then it's a good thing you're kneeling down." Narrowing her eyes, in a serious blunt tone, she said, "Your grandpa lied to you. Mason, I'm not going to sugarcoat this. You need to know the truth. Your parents weren't missionaries. They were drug addicts."

Mason's jaw dropped and his stomach tightened and ached as if he'd been punched there. The air rushed from his lungs. At first, his throat choked off his words, but he did manage a weak, "What?"

"Mason, listen to me. I know how unbelievable this sounds, but it's the truth, every word. My husband and I were dear friends with your grandpa. He was like a brother to me. We shared everything. One night he confessed that your dad and mom had voluntarily entered rehab for their addiction to heroin. They ended up going several times. And, they ran into some trouble with the law and spent some time in jail. Your grandpa bankrupted himself, trying to get them both clean for you. He second mortgaged his farm, and ended up losing it. Honey, do you remember the last time you saw your parents?"

Mason nodded, blankly staring ahead. "Yeah, they dropped me off at my grandpa's trailer and told me they were going to Mexico for a week. But never came back." His heart sunk as he realized she was telling him the truth. "Do you think they were ever going to come back?"

"Honest? No," Pauline answered. "I think they were on the run when they left. I don't have any proof, just a guess."

"People in town have always been nice to me, most at least. Why the sudden change?"

"Because *now* everyone knows what I just told you. Until early this morning, no one knew."

"I don't understand."

"Your grandpa did a near impossible job keeping your parents' troubles secret. Only a few of us knew, and we kept quiet to protect you."

"Who told everyone?"

"I don't know. A text message was sent to some members of the church congregation. From there, the gossip spread like wildfire burning dry brush."

"I still don't understand. People know me. They know I'm not a drug addict."

"Whoever told everyone about your dad and mom said you're just like them."

"But that's not true."

"I know, dearheart. Some people, though, can be very convincing, and very cruel."

Chapter Six

Mason spent his restless Saturday night hiding at home, away from everyone. When Sunday morning came he turned on the television and watched an old movie instead of attending morning mass. He wanted to go but feared how the people at church might shun him. Soon enough he would know for sure. By now, everyone should have heard the rumors about his parents. Heartbroken by how they suffered from their addiction, his sadness and anger over their leaving him made him question if they ever did love him.

He'd tossed and turned on the couch, missing his friend, Jared. Saturday nights had usually been spent riding around, listening to music on the radio and talking about nothing important. This was their American dream. Mason's thoughts alternated between missing Jared and Scarlett and her son. There was no denying his attraction to her and how much he liked holding and taking care of her son. As impossible as it sounded, he wondered, *is it possible to fall in love by just meeting someone? I hope it is. I've never felt this way before, and I don't want it to stop.*

A few hours later, Mason stood outside Scarlett's motel room door. He'd tried twice knocking, but his hand shook too much. Nervousness over their date, and what people in town now thought of him spoiled his hopes for the afternoon. Scared she wouldn't want to be seen with him after finding out the rumors, he knew he'd be devastated if she rejected him. Not one for ever being able to tell a lie or keep a secret, he wanted to be truthful with her, even if it meant she'd tell him good-bye.

His third attempt to knock halted when she opened the door. The butterflies in his stomach surged with her smiling at him.

"My, don't you look handsome," she complimented him.

"It's just jeans and a blue denim shirt, nothing special," he responded. "That is a real pretty dress you're wearing," he returned her compliment. "The green matches the color of your eyes."

"Thank you."

Losing his nerves, Mason uttered, "Hey, listen… um… there's something… I need to tell you."

Scarlett reached out and took hold of his hand. "I already know, and I don't believe a word of it."

Though still anxious, some relief flooded through him as he released his breath. "How did you find out?"

"The woman who manages this place, Miss Durkin, warned me about you."

"I'll understand if you don't want to be seen with me."

Stepping closer to him, with her other hand she caressed his cheek. "The *only* thing I want is to be seen with you."

"Are you sure? The stuff being said about me and my parents is pretty bad."

"I don't care what they're saying. I can't think of another man I'd want taking Kyle and me to a church social."

"So, you still want to go? We could do something else."

"No. We *need* to go to the church social. You gotta to show them their hateful rumors about you are no more than terrible lies. You need to be fearless. You aren't your parents."

Mason felt his throat grow dry as looked down and forced out, "What if I can't be fearless?"

"Then you take hold of my hand, and I'll give you my courage."

"They used to be my friends. Now I don't know that I can face those people."

"Yes, you can. You're going to hold your head up high and remind them of who you are."

"Who am I?"

Scarlett kissed his cheek and answered, "A good man, one of the best I think."

***

Scarlett looked up at the sky and commented, "This may be the Summer Solstice, but I don't think we'll see much sun today."

Mason glanced out toward the wide open western horizon, noticing how dark the blue sky appeared. "Yeah, we're gonna get a storm, a pretty bad one I think."

Kyle began fussing for Scarlett. "May I hold him?" Mason asked.

"Yes, you can. I believe he likes you. What's not to like?" Her last words caused Mason to blush as he took and held him up to his shoulder. His fussing lasted only another minute before finding a comfortable spot to rest his head.

"He's a good boy," Mason whispered as he ran his fingers through Kyle's wispy hair.

Behind the church, booths for children's games, a bake sale, and tables were set up. The pleasant smell of barbeque chicken and hamburgers sizzling on a grill was carried by strong breezes. Everyone in town seemed to be here, wandering around, enjoying the fellowship of the gathering.

Corrupting the spirit of this happy event were the not-too-subtle stares and whispers passing between several when they noticed Mason standing there. Scarlett was right, this would be awkward. Mason offered greetings to several who acted as if they hadn't heard him. The lack of acknowledgment and coldness of these people surprised her. *They know Mason. My goodness, how quickly they've turned on him, all because of the hateful rumors. How can they be so cruel?*

"Are you sure you want to stay?" Mason mumbled under his breath after being ignored by another couple.

Furious, though hiding it with a smile, Scarlett responded, "We are staying, if for no other reason than to make them pay for how badly they're treating you. You two wait here. I'm going to get us some lemonade."

Scarlett recognized the woman pouring drinks. She had been the one who took her money to get into the drive-in movie. "Hello," Scarlett greeted her. "May I have two cups of lemonade?" The woman nodded her head and handed the cups to her.

Speaking softly, the woman warned, "I don't think it's wise for you to be spending time with Mason. Yes, he's handsome and all, but there are troubling things about him we've just learned."

"What did you learn, and who did you learn it from?"

Clearly startled by Scarlett's stern attitude, the woman answered, "I'm not at liberty to say."

"Overnight, the nicest young man has gone from being a favorite in town to not being welcome. He has the right to know why."

"It's complicated," the woman offered, glancing slightly away.

"It's mean." Scarlett continued, challenging, "Look at Mason. He's still as sweet and gentle as he was yesterday. All of you have harshly judged and juried him because of who his parents were and the problems they had. He is neither of them. Mason is a good you man. You know I'm right."

"I don't want to believe any of it," the woman quietly confessed.

"Then don't. Just look in those pretty blue eyes of his, and you'll see how heartbroken he is. Please, don't make him suffer for stuff he didn't do. He isn't his mom and dad."

The woman's chin quivered as she was overwhelmed with emotions. Taking a deep breath, she walked over to Mason and surprised him by kissing his cheek and grabbing his hand. The chilled attitudes of those standing near soon disappeared. Each offered him the warm greeting he was denied when they arrived. Smiles and pats on the back replaced cold stares and whispers.

Scarlett handed him his cup of lemonade.

"Whatever you said to her, thank you," he said.

"She just needed reminding of what she already knew. They all did."

Hearing a favorite song of hers being played on the radio, Scarlett asked, "May I have this dance?"

Mason grinned and answered, "This and every other dance."

They set their lemonades down, and Scarlett wrapped her arm around his waist as they slowly danced to the melody. Kyle never stirred, resting his sleeping angelic face against Mason. "*Strawberry Wine* is my favorite song," she said. "I remember the first time I danced to it. It was with a boy who I had a wonderful crush on."

"What was his name?"

"Mason," she answered, causing him to smile and blush.

Continuing to sway to the music, Mason looked closer at her wrist and complimented her. "That's a pretty rose tattoo you have there."

"Thank you. Now, I've seen you shirtless but didn't notice any tattoos on you. Anything you're hiding?" she playfully asked.

"No, I was born perfect. A tattoo would just be showing off," he joked.

Scarlett shook her head. "I think you could drive me crazy." Mason grinned.

"I bet your smile melts lots of hearts."

"I'm only interested in melting one." Looking down at Kyle, he changed this to, "Two, really."

A strong gust of wind and the distant sound of rolling thunder stopped their dance.

The church pastor called out, "*Everyone*, if we could have some volunteers, we need to move all this down to the social room in the church basement. A storm is coming. Once we get all this down there, Mrs. Shannon will be calling out the bingo numbers."

Mason gentle handed Kyle back to Scarlett and rushed off to help the others move the food and games down to the basement. She kissed Kyle's head as she watched the darkening sky. A strong, heated gust of air blew her hair, and her jaw dropped when a bolt of lighting passed from one cloud to the next. "Don't you worry none," she whispered to Kyle. "We'll be safe inside."

Not yet ready to go down to the basement, Scarlett held Kyle close and walked with him up around the front of the church. "Wow," she uttered, looking to the west, seeing a massive storm cloud and birds soaring in the intense gusts of wind. A sign out front was wrenched from the ground and landed at her feet. She picked it up and read, "Help wanted."

Before she could find someone to give it to, Scarlett noticed an argument between a police officer and a woman. The woman appeared to want to leave, but the police officer was insisting she stay. Her attention was drawn away from this, though, when another woman asked, "Are you interested in the job?"

***

"Have you ever won at bingo?" Scarlett asked.

"Not once," Mason answered but then added, "My luck might be changing, though. I just need two more numbers."

"B seven," Mrs. Shannon called out.

"Got it," Mason said, covering the number on his card. "I just need one more."

The overhead lights flickered, causing gasps from a few people. Across the room, the pastor had gathered the kids for quiet Bible story reading time. On the other side of the room, a group of men were huddled around the radio, listening to a sports broadcaster and commenting on his reports. Mostly women and teens were sitting and playing bingo at several lined tables.

"G sixty," Mrs. Shannon said.

Scarlett looked around and could tell by the reactions of at least three people, they were close to winning. An older woman shushed some teens who were talking too loud. They quieted down a little, but not enough to the woman's liking. She huffed her frustration and warned them again, this time with a cold glance.

"G sixty-two."

"Bingo!" Mason called out. He waved his hand, and Mrs. Shannon walked over to check his card. His excitement caused her to laugh.

"It's a good bingo, folks. Mason is the winner," she said and smiled at him. Handing him his winnings, fifty dollars, she lowered her voice and offered, "I'm so sorry about what happened earlier today. My husband feels terrible about it too. I hope you'll accept our apology."

Mason looked her in the eye and smiled and nodded. "I do."

Mrs. Shannon patted his hand and returned to the table to call out numbers for the next game.

"Here," Mason said, handing the fifty dollars to Scarlett.

She refused to take it. "That belongs to you. I can't."

"I think you need it more than I do."

"We'll be fine."

"Please, take it," he urged.

"No, as I said, we'll be fine."

Mason frowned and shoved the money into his pocket. "I know it's none of my business, but...what are you gonna do?"

Scarlett sighed. "I spoke to my dad. Tomorrow morning he's wiring money to me for bus tickets for us to go back to Fargo. He claims it's the Christian thing to do. I guess once we're back there, I'll see if it works out."

"What if it doesn't?"

"Then I'll have to come up with something else."

"Is that really what you want to do, go back to Fargo?"

"No, I mean I don't know. A part of me hopes I can work things out with my parents. Maybe when they see me with Kyle, they'll change their minds and welcome us both home."

"I can't see anyone not loving that sweet little boy," Mason said, glancing over her shoulder at Kyle in his stroller.

Appreciating the growing bond between Mason and Kyle, Scarlett wondered, *will I ever find another man like him? I've never met someone so sweet and kind.*

Scarlett was startled when Mason suggested, "Maybe... you both don't have to leave."

"What do you mean?"

He looked nervous as he continued, "Well, you both could stay with me, I mean stay at my trailer. Gosh, that doesn't sound too appealing, does it? Look, I know I don't have much to offer...but it could be home. It is for me. Yeah, it's small, but there's enough room. You could sleep in the bedroom, and we could set Kyle up in the bunk area."

"And where would you sleep?"

"Oh, don't worry about me. I always fall asleep on the couch, listening to the radio or watching TV." He swallowed, summoning his courage. "I would take good care of you both."

"I know you would," Scarlett responded, brushing strands of hair away from her eyes. "I appreciate the offer. It's real nice of you."

"But you won't stay."

Feeling a little ashamed, Scarlett glanced away, saying, "No, I can't. I need to go back to Fargo and try to work things out with my parents. I'm sorry."

Mason shook his head and tried smiling. "There's nothing to be sorry about. I understand."

Seeing a dessert table, and needing to step away so she wouldn't break down and cry in front of him, Scarlett forced a smile and said, "I'm going to get us some pie. What kind do you want?"

"Apple, please," Mason answered.

Of course, you do. That's what I would expect the perfect boy next door to eat.

Chapter Seven

From the corner of her eye, Scarlett saw Mason put his fifty dollars in Kyle's diaper bag. *Oh, no you don't,* she thought. *That belongs to you. From what I've overheard others say, you need it as much as I do.*

When she returned with a plate of pie in each hand, Scarlett saw Kyle beginning to fuss.

"Do you want me to hold him?" Mason asked.

What I really want you to do is hold me, Scarlett said in her mind. *But I can't let that happen. I can't lead you on and then let you go. It's already too hard to look at you, and I don't want to do anything else but that.*

"No, I'll take him upstairs for a few minutes until he calms down. Play my bingo card for the next game. Maybe you'll bring me luck, and I'll win something too."

"Okay."

She carried Kyle up the steps and into the church sanctuary. Subtle rattles echoed through the old country church. She looked out the front door and saw two small trees being bent by the force of the wind. It hadn't rained yet which surprised her. But a loud clap of thunder and a burst of lightning told her, the storm was bearing down on them.

Wandering up the main church aisle to the altar, she admired two solid white statues of the Virgin Mary and Jesus. An ornately, hand carved wooden cross hung on the far wall and paintings of angels adorned the plastered ceiling.

Kyle had stopped his fussing and was looking at her with sleepy eyes. She swayed a little as she stood there, lured into a daydream.

"This pretty little church is the kind of place I want to get married in someday," she whispered to him. "My wedding dress will be white and have lots of lace. And my bouquet will be wild daisies. You will be my ring bearer, walking down the aisle with the prettiest little flower girl. I'll be walked down the aisle by my dad to the man of my dreams, just like the one sitting downstairs playing bingo. He'll be wearing a gray tuxedo and a white linen shirt. He'll smile when he sees me for the first time in my dress, and I'll lose my breath by how handsome he is."

A powerful, loud tremor shook the floor under them. She was mistaken, thinking, *a train must be running nearby*. It was too late when she realized she was wrong.

The sound of a shattering window caused her to scream, startling Kyle. She tried to hush his crying, turning around to see a stop sign the wind had pierced a stained-glass window with. The howling gusts shook everything in sight, blowing songbooks off the pews and hurling them against the wall. Part of the roof above the pulpit was wrenched away, damaging the painted angel, decorating the plaster there.

Knowing it wasn't safe to stay in the sanctuary, Scarlett rushed with Kyle in her arms over to the basement door. She lacked the strength, though, to move the stop sign out of the way. The force of the wind blowing through the shattered window nearly knocked her off her feet. Seeing two more windows shatter, Scarlett moved to the center aisle, looking for a place to shield herself and Kyle. The rows of pews were bolted to the floor. Pushed by the intense wind, she stumbled over to one and wedged herself and Kyle underneath the seat. Covering his head with her hands, "Dear God," was all she could utter as Kyle cried in her trembling arms.

***

The continuous flickering and buzzing of the church basement lights caused several gasps from those gathered. Mason kept his eyes on the entrance to the staircase leading up to the sanctuary, waiting for Scarlett and Kyle to return. After one last flicker, the lights went out, and he bolted from his seat toward the entrance. The basement had become pitch-black, and he collided with someone before walking into the wall. Rubbing his shoulder from the impact, he traced his hand along the brick wall until finding the steps. He looked up the darkened stairwell and noticed a thin sliver of light penetrating through a gap.

His heart wedged in his throat as he climbed to the door. By the time he reached for the doorknob, his hand was shaking. It turned with ease, but the door only opened an inch. It was blocked on the other side by something. Through the open space, he yelled, "Scarlett!" Over the howling wind, he heard no response from her.

Adrenalized with fear, he struggled to force the door open a few more inches. Still not able to push it open enough to get through, he thought of calling down for help. A loud crash from inside the church, though, made him panic. Slamming his body several times against the door, it opened a few more inches, enough for him to slip through.

Almost all the stain-glass windows had been shattered, coating the hardwood floor with sparkling, colorful shards of glass. The walls and most of the church ceiling remained intact though the walls bowed and the wood in many places had splintered.

Panting to catch his breath, he looked all around for them and worried, *did they run outside. Dear God, where are you? Please be safe.*

Stepping into the main aisle, the sounds of the wind and echoing thunder deafened him. His heart stopped with his next step taken, when he felt something grab his leg. He glanced down to see Scarlett's frightened face looking up at him. Relief flooded him, and he wanted to pull her and Kyle out from under the pew and help them down to the basement. A loud crash behind him stopped this. A beam had fallen, cutting off their escape. Knowing what he needed to do, Mason knelt and covered Scarlett and Kyle with his body. Not once did he take his eyes off them, staring at the terror on Scarlett's expression, hoping he could hide his fear for their sake.

***

Never before had Scarlett been blessed to have someone willingly sacrifice anything for her, not even her parents, and definitely not Clint. Mason hardly knew her yet would put himself in harm's way to keep her and Kyle safe. This made the growing love she felt for him all the stronger.

Mason's neck and shoulder muscles flexed as the debris fell on him, his face revealed the strain. Fearing the end was near for all of them, she gave in to a craving she couldn't, nor wanted to stop. She leaned up and kissed his lips. Looking into his eyes, she found no hesitation. If anything, she recognized how much stronger he seemed, as if he had drawn courage from her. Mason mouthed words to her. The heavy wind and Kyle's wailing made her ears pound. She couldn't hear his voice but knew what he said. *I love you.*

A large piece of wood fell across his back, causing him to groan in pain. The skin on his face turned beet red, and she watched his jaw clamp down, his teeth grinding. He defied his distressed breaths and shaking body as he held on. *If this is the end, I'm happy he's here with us*, Scarlett thought. *It just isn't long enough.*

As fast as the storm had struck, that is how quickly it faded away. The air felt heavy and much cooler as the winds bearing down on the church lessened. Mason struggled to stand, and after looking around, he reached down for her. Once on her feet, he held both her and Kyle close as they stood in the ruins of the sanctuary. Kyle's crying stopped when Mason took him from her arms, leaving only the sound of the church bell ringing out from the tower. For the most part, much of the church had survived the storm.

As Mason turned around, Scarlett's jaw dropped. The fabric of his wind-torn denim shirt was slashed across his back. Red blood stains discolored it from his neck to his waist. "You're hurt," she fretted.

"I'm okay. It only stings a little," he responded.

Liar, she said to herself.

Hearing sirens in the distance, she followed Mason as he pushed through the debris to the church's missing front door where outside shingles from the church roof fluttered to the ground like autumn leaves. She noticed the clearing sky and shafts of sunlight piercing the remaining cloud cover above the expansive wide open. The actual storm was over, but an emotional one lay ready to strike.

***

As paramedics tended to the cuts and bruises covering Mason's back, Scarlett asked, "How much damage did the twister do to the town?"

"It wasn't a twister," one of the EMT's answered. "It's called a dry microburst. It can act like a twister, but in truth is just nasty wind. The town got spared, pretty much. The church here and the drive-in just up the road took the worst of it."

"Are you sure you don't want to go to the hospital?" the second EMT asked Mason. "I'd feel better if we got some X-rays of your ribs. Those are some nasty bruises you got."

"I'm okay," Mason insisted. "Just bandage me up and send me on my way."

"Was anyone else hurt?" she asked.

"Luckily, no," the first EMT said.

Mason groaned a little as he unsteadily stood. "I should take you and Kyle home...if I knew where my truck was."

"Is it that one over in the tree?" the second EMT asked and pointed.

"Yeah, that's it," Sheriff Crawford answered for him. He approached the ambulance and offered, "I'll drive the three of you home. Mason, I'll write out a report for the insurance, and you can sign it the

next time you're by the police station."
Mason nodded his head.

"I don't have a car seat for Kyle. It's in Mason's truck. The motel isn't far. I have his stroller, so I'll just push him in that and walk back to the motel."

"Mason, I'll drive you home," the sheriff insisted. "You're in no shape to walk that far."

"Yes, Sir."

"Come on."

"I'll be there in a minute," Mason said, looking at Scarlett.

"I'll wait over there for you," Sheriff Crawford responded.

Once alone, Mason leaned over and kissed Kyle's head. "Don't you give your mom too much trouble tonight."

"He'll be fine."

"And, what about you?"

"I'll be fine too," she answered, forcing a smile on her face. He nodded and took a step back but stopped when she asked, "Why did you say you loved me?"

"Because I do," he answered with no hesitation. "The first time I saw you, I knew. I guess that sounds pretty stupid. I don't even really know you."

"It's not stupid," she insisted. "It's sweet. Don't regret saying it."

Mason sighed and tried to smile. Scarlett smiled back until he asked, "Why did you kiss me? I'm glad you did."

"I thought we were going to die. I couldn't imagine dying without kissing you."

"Thank you."

"For what?"

"It's... I..." he struggled and then finally said, "It's been a long day. I needed to hear that."

He took another step back and again stopped. "Maybe if things don't work out in Fargo, you might want to come back here. I meant what I said, everything," he offered.

"And I meant it when I kissed you." Sighing and trying to smile, she swallowed hard and added, "I don't like saying good-bye, so I'll just say good night."

"Good night, Scarlett."

Chapter Eight

The whole time driving to his trailer, not once did Sheriff Crawford say anything. When he pulled into the dark driveway, he turned off the engine, and they sat there in silence. Before Mason could thank him for the ride home, the sheriff said, "My wife left me today." Mason stayed quiet as Sheriff Crawford continued, "she told me she came on to you, and that you rejected her. Thank you."

"I'm sorry," Mason offered.

"You didn't do anything wrong. You're a good man, unlike me. I'd known for a long time how unhappy she was. I knew a bunch of secrets she kept hidden. I just wanted to make it work here. I wanted her to be happy, but I couldn't make that happen."

"So, what are you gonna do?"

"I'm letting her go. She's on her way back to Kansas City. That's where we met. We got married there a year after our first date. A year after that something happened, I begged her to leave and come out here to the wide open with me."

"What happened?"

"I was on patrol one night when I came across a young man, about your age, breaking into a store. He must have been using drugs by all the marks on his arms. Anyway, he was crashing off them and in need of a fix. He was trying to steal money to buy more drugs, but I stopped him. We wrestled on the ground while he was resisting arrest. He got a hold of my gun and held it to my head. When he pressed the trigger, somehow it jammed. But when he turned the barrel around, the gun discharged and sent a bullet through his head. He died before he hit the ground. After that, I couldn't go back out on patrol. All I saw was his face. Sometimes, I still see it. That's what makes what I'm about to tell you all the harder."

"How?"

"My wife hacked my computer. She was the one who got information on you which she spread around town. She was bitter that you rejected her and wanted to punish you. I know what she told people. There was a part, though, she held back. It's this part you need to know now. After all these years, I think you deserve the whole truth."

"About what?"

"What do you remember about the last time you saw your parents?"

Mason thought for a minute and answered, "Before they dropped me off at my grandpa's trailer, I remembered us stopping at the gas station for a soda."

"Were either of them acting strange?"

"Yeah, my dad was, maybe my mom too. My dad was nervous. He didn't like flying, and they were leaving for a mission trip to Mexico. I know that's not true now. They were in trouble with the law. Drugs I guess."

"That was part of it," Sheriff Crawford confirmed. "What you don't know is how they were going to pay for those drugs and their airplane tickets to Mexico. From the police reports, your dad had contacted someone about selling you. That was how they were going to pay for what they wanted."

Mason shook his head. "No, they wouldn't have done that. They loved me."

"They loved the drugs more. I'm sorry, Mason. I wouldn't lie to you. It's the truth."

Feeling as if he'd been punched in the stomach, Mason swallowed hard as he felt his body trembling. He tried asking a question. All that came out was a soft-spoken, "How?"

"Unknown to them, the man your dad contacted was an agent for the FBI."

Tears stung Mason's eyes as he sat there quietly. His heart sank, reeling as he tried to deal with what he was hearing. *My dad wanted to sell me for drugs. It was always about getting high, never about me. I've wasted years believing they loved me and they'd come back for me. I feel so stupid. Damn.*

"Do you know where my parents are?"

"Yeah, I do." Exhaling, Sheriff Crawford revealed, "About three years ago, just outside Wheeling, West Virginia, your mom was found unresponsive in a homeless shelter. Paramedics tried to revive her. She ended up dying of a heroin overdose. As for your dad, he's serving a life sentence in a Florida maximum security prison for killing a man. I'm sorry."

Unable to hold in his emotions, Mason burst into tears.

"Come here," Sheriff Crawford urged. Mason leaned over so the sheriff could hug him. "I'm sorry," he repeated. "Mason, listen to me. You are a fine young man. I would be proud to have a son like you. Don't believe they didn't love you.

Addiction is a disease they couldn't cure themselves of. It destroyed them. It doesn't have to do that to you, even though it may feel that way."

Mason pulled away, wiping the tears from his face. He nodded to the sheriff and reached for the door handle. At first, he couldn't open it, but on the second try, he did.

"Do you want me to stay here with you for a little while? Trust me. I'm in no hurry to go home to an empty house."

Mason sat there, thinking, *this is the first time I've ever felt alone out here in the wide open. Even after Grandpa died, I didn't feel this way. I'm scared to walk in there by myself.*

"I could use the company," Mason responded.

"So could I."

***

Scarlett rolled over and looked at Kyle. He was sound asleep next to her there on the floor. She looked up at the ceiling fan, the blades rotating slow, stirring the warm air in the room, offering no cooling comfort.

Growing restless, careful not to wake Kyle, she stood up and tiptoed to the door leading outside. The blacktop parking lot radiated heat against the soles of her bare feet. After the storm, the air had cooled, but it proved only a brief respite from the sweltering heat gripping North Dakota.

She looked up at an endless array of stars, hoping to find one shooting across the sky. Though the notion was silly, she wanted to make a wish and hoped it would come true. Many times she'd heard of others wishing on a star so they could be with the one they loved. With her twentieth birthday only a month away, she knew she shouldn't believe in such foolish little girl ideas. But her rebellious nature had robbed her of some of her youth. *I don't regret what's happened and wouldn't change a thing. If I did, Kyle wouldn't be here with me. I can't imagine my life without him. I'm gonna be the best mom he could ever hope for and try hard to give him the life he deserves. Where will that be?*

I don't want to go home... but I don't have a choice, she thought. With no money left, and no means to care for Kyle, she couldn't reject her dad's offer to wire money to her for bus tickets back to Fargo. "We'll talk things through when you get home," he told her. What does that mean? In the past when he said this, it meant *I'm going to tell you what to do, and you'd do best to listen.* Her life wasn't as simple as it used to be. *It's not just me anymore.*

Needing to clear her mind, Scarlett thought of Mason, which ended up being a mistake. In such a short time, she found herself attracted to more than just his handsome features. *He's the sweetest man I've ever met, selfless, kind, sincere. I'm not sure I'll ever find anyone like him again. Maybe after Kyle and I leave, I can keep in touch with him.*

Leaving, why can't I stop thinking about that? I can't stay... but I don't want to leave.

Scarlett looked up just in time to see a shooting star streak across the dark sky. Despite what she thought earlier, with no hesitation, she said, "I wish I knew what to do?"

***

"I'm sorry. I don't have any beer to offer you," Mason said to Sheriff Crawford.

Sitting down across the small table from him, the sheriff responded, "Don't be sorry. After what I saw recently, I don't think I'll ever drink again."

"What did you see?"

"A young guy, about your age, got drunk and wrecked his Mustang. From what I can tell he was going about eighty miles per hour when he lost control. I'm pretty sure he was killed instantly."

"That's too bad. Was he from around here?"

"I don't think so. To be honest, there wasn't much left of either him or his car. I ran the plates through the license bureau and found out the car was stolen. I might not find out who the driver was until the county coroner finishes his examination of the body."

For a moment both were gripped with an awkward silence until Mason said, "I still feel bad about you and your wife."

"It's not your fault. It's mine."

"Do you think she got caught in the storm?"

"I don't know. I haven't heard from her, and I don't think I will. To be honest, I'm surprised you're concerned about her, considering what she did to you."

Mason shrugged his shoulders.

"What about that girl and her son you were with today at the picnic?"

Mason glanced down and answered, "They're just passing through. They're leaving tomorrow."

"Something tells me that's not what you want."

"It isn't, but they can't stay."

"I'm sorry."

"Me too."

"Considering what I told you about your parents, and her leaving, and how you were treated today, you've had a really bad day."

"Yeah."

After another minute of silence passed, Mason asked, "Do you think my dad would talk to me if I tried contacting him?"

"Son, listen to me. My best advice would be *not* to talk to him. I understand why you might want to, but he knows where you're at and hasn't made any effort to talk to you. I can't see anything good coming from you wanting to connect with him. In the end, it's your decision. I just don't want to see you more heartbroken than you already are."

Mason shifted in his seat and winced from the pain of his injuries.

"Come on. You need to lie down. I'll help you to your bedroom."

"No, I'd rather lay down on the couch."

"Okay." Mason stood up and walked over to the couch. Turning onto his stomach, the sheriff covered him with a blanket. "I'll let you get some sleep."

"You could stay longer if you want. One of the late west coast baseball games might still be on the radio."

"Okay," Sheriff Crawford sat down in an easy chair next to the couch and turned on the radio. The eighth inning of the Giant's game against the Cardinal's had just started. After the second out, the sheriff said, "I hear you're one of the best carpenters in town."

"I guess I'm pretty good with wood and tools. My grandpa taught me a lot before he died."

"I need a carpenter. I've got a job that will pay real good."

"Doing what?"

"I want to renovate my house. I know my wife isn't coming back. I don't want any reminders of her. Every room in my house is going to be how *I* want it. I'll be around to help as much as I can. If you want the job, it's yours once you feel up to it."

"Yes, Sir. I'm sure I could make it just the way you want."

"Good."

"Thanks."

The sheriff smiled and nodded his head. The two sat there, quietly listening to the rest of the baseball game until Mason's eyes grew too heavy to stay open.

Chapter Nine

Scarlett carried Kyle outside to look at the morning sky and secured him in his stroller. Shades of pink, pale orange, blue, and violet blended together for the most beautiful sky she'd ever seen. *It's like a bunch of pastel-colored crayons melted in the first beam of light. I bet the sky has always been this breathtaking*, she thought. *I've just haven't taken the time to look at it.* "What a wonderful day this could be," she said to Kyle. "It would be even better if we could stay."

She'd hoped Mason would be waiting outside her door when she opened it. Her heart sank when he wasn't there. During the night she thought about keeping in touch with him after she left. She realized, though, she didn't have his phone number and didn't know where he lived. *That was stupid of me not to ask him for his number or where he lived.* Sighing, she thought, *Maybe, it's better this way. As much as I want to see him again, it would be too hard to say good-bye.* Her chin quivered and tears stung her eyes. She tried to pull herself together even though she was close to falling apart.

Struggling to carry her suitcase and diaper bag as she pushed Kyle in his stroller, she stopped at the motel office and turned in her room key. Then they headed for the post office where her dad said he'd wire the money to her for the bus tickets. She was kind of happy it took a long time to walk down the street. There was no hurry to face going back to Fargo.

As they passed by a few storefront windows, Scarlett stopped to look at the items on display. An antique shop had old glassware pieces that reminded her of things she'd seen at her grandma's house when she was little. Looking further into the shop, she saw an old bicycle and several tables littered with stuff to buy.

Next to this was a beauty shop. The hairdresser was coloring a lady's hair. She thought they might be gossiping by the way they moved their hands, covering their mouths, pointing and nodding. A flatbed tow truck driving slowly behind her appeared in the glass window's reflection. It was carrying pieces of a severely damaged car. For a moment, there was something familiar about the car that struck her. Kyle's fussing pulled her thoughts away from the tow truck, letting go of what she knew was unimportant.

Reaching the post office, she read the sign, "Open in a half hour." *What should we do now?* She remembered the church being close and decided to walk in that direction. The gaping hole in the roof had been covered by a tarp, and the shattered windows were boarded up. Other than some missing white aluminum siding, it didn't look as bad as it did last night.

Again, her thoughts returned to Mason, thinking of how he protected them during the storm. *I can't thank him enough for what he did for us.* Once more, she agonized, *I wish I could tell him good-bye, and I wish I didn't have to.*

As she turned around to leave, a familiar woman approached her and asked, "So, did you give it any thought?"

***

Mason woke up, hearing the rumble of Mister Shannon's tractor. Looking around, he found himself lying on his stomach on the couch. The radio volume had been turned down, just loud enough to know it was still on. Sheriff Crawford was gone. He didn't remember him leaving. They had talked for a while after he'd drove him home. He remembered the sheriff offered him a good-paying carpentry job, helping to renovate his home. He wanted to get rid of all traces of his wife. *He offered to help me with the work. Probably doesn't want to be alone. Neither do I.*

Mason glanced over at his grandpa's empty chair. On the lamp table next to it was the book he'd been reading and his glasses. *Did you know what happened to them? Was this something else you kept from me? I guess I understand why you did. I'm not mad at you. If you see Mom, tell her I'm okay if she hasn't been watching me. I'm not angry at her or Dad. The sheriff and I talked about him. I know where he is, but I'm not going to try to talk to him. He's gone and is never coming back. Someday when I'm a dad, I'll try to be a better one than him.*

Struggling to stand, the pain and stiffness of his back made it hard to breathe for a moment. He went to the bathroom and glanced at his tired reflection in the mirror. He wasn't really looking at himself though. All he could see was Scarlett and Kyle. Again, he had difficulty breathing, but not because of his injuries. His heart ached, knowing they would be gone soon.

He ran his hand over the stubble on his cheek and chin. He needed a shave. The will to do so wasn't there. Removing his bandages and taking off his jeans, he stepped into the shower and turned on the faucet. The warm water stung his cuts, and he cursed a few times. He couldn't help it. After dressing, he walked out to the kitchen and poured a bowl of cereal. He took a bite but realized he wasn't hungry. It was something he just did every day when he got up. He walked over to the couch and folded his blanket, again following what he normally did. *I don't want to repeat doing things the same way, one day after another. I guess I'm not the same man I was yesterday.*

Checking the time on the wall-mounted clock, he thought of Scarlett and Kyle. *They get picked up by the bus in an hour at the edge of town. I know it's stupid to think this since I've only just met them, but I love them both. I wish they would stay.* These last words kept repeating in his mind until he decided, *Maybe I should try again? Maybe she won't leave if I ask her one more time to stay. I can't lose someone else I love. I'm not strong enough for that.*

He went outside and remembered his truck in the tree next to the church. He looked at his bicycle, realizing he hadn't changed the flat tire yet. Sighing deep, he mumbled, "I guess I'm walking."

Unlike yesterday, the sky had turned the right kind of blue for a beautiful day. A white cloud passed in front of the sun, sending a shadow across the plush, windblown fields as far as his eyes could see. Only the sound of his shoes scraping against the dirt road corrupted the peaceful silence. His pace was slower than usual with his back throbbing with each step.

The mile walk to where the bus stopped gave Mason the chance to think about all that had happened. *I don't want to be alone anymore. Grandpa's gone and Mom and Dad aren't ever coming back. Jared, too. I never thought of the wide open as being lonely, but now, it's too quiet.*

Some crows landed on a fence near where he walked. They squawked at him. *"Yeah, yeah, even the birds are telling me how stupid I am. By the time I get to the bus stop, they'll be gone. I don't even have a phone number to call her and don't know where her parents live in Fargo. I should stop walking and go home.* He didn't.

From behind him, he heard what sounded like a truck approaching. It slowed down as it reached him. It didn't come to a complete stop. From the corner of his eye, he recognized the color of the truck and knew it belonged to Jared's dad. Mason waited for him to call out his open passenger-side window. He wasn't really surprised when he didn't. Jared's dad had slowed his truck's speed to a crawl, matching Mason's pace. A minute later he floored it, leaving behind a wake of dust and flying stones, one of which struck Mason's leg. He cursed under his breath and rubbed the spot on his thigh where the stone hit.

A few minutes later, a cloud of swirling dust from the intersection down the road made him stop walking. He knew he was too late. The bus pulled away. There was no use running, not that he could anyway with the pain radiating from his back. His heart sank. They were gone.

Instead of turning back, Mason kept walking to the intersection. By the time he reached it, most of the dust had settled. He looked right and caught the last glimpse of the bus before it was out of sight. The sound of a car pulling up to him pulled his attention away from this.

"Can I give you a ride?" an elderly gentleman asked.

For a split second he thought, *could you help me catch that bus*, but instead responded, "No, Sir. Thanks anyway."

He stepped back and watched the man drive away in his old red sedan. *They're gone, like everyone else.* Kicking the dirt, he kept thinking, *maybe I should just keep walking. I don't know if I can go home.*

He took a step forward but stopped. A stray breeze caressed his cheek. The feeling of this reminded him of his mom touching his face when she tucked him in bed at night. She knew he feared monsters under his bed. She'd always tell him, "Don't be afraid. You're not alone."

He let out a deep breath. As he turned to walk home, he heard Scarlett say, "I couldn't leave. I hoped you would come and stop me."

Left speechless and feeling the butterflies surge in his stomach, he watched her approach him. He'd been looking at the bus leaving and didn't notice her standing there. Kyle's little head was resting on her shoulder, and his eyes were open, staring at him.

"Does your offer still stand? Could Kyle and I stay with you?"

Swallowing hard, Mason answered, "Yeah, if you want to."

"I do."

"Okay."

"But we need to settle a few things."

"Like what?"

She smiled and responded, "I took the part-time receptionist job at the church. It's only twenty hours a week, but I can take Kyle with me. It's not a lot of money. I insist on helping pay for some of the bills."

"I don't want you to do that. I'm guessing I can't stop you," Mason responded.

"I won't take no for an answer."

"Okay."

Scarlett brushed windblown strands of her hair away from her face and smiled even bigger at him. "I... well... I think you could be the man of my dreams, the man I could be in love with, the man I'm already in love with. I just want, no I need to take this slow. I don't want to rush this."

"Yeah," he agreed.

"I want to learn everything there is to know about you and for you to know everything about me. I want to know what you're like when you're grumpy and I want you to tell me all there is to know about you, from your favorite book and color to the flavor of ice cream you like."

"Chocolate chip," he interrupted and grinned. "Sorry, that's moving too fast."

"You are gonna drive me crazy, aren't you?"

His grin changed to a beaming smile as he said, "Sorry."

"No, you're not."

"No, I'm not."

"Good, I don't want there to be any lies between us."

"There won't be. I promise."

Her son began squirming in her arms. Scarlett smiled and offered, "I think Kyle wants you to hold him."

Mason eased Kyle off her shoulder and held him to his own. His tiny fingers stroked the fabric of Mason's white T-shirt.

"Thank you," Mason said as Scarlett reached out and touched the hand holding Kyle.

"For what?"

He swallowed hard and felt a tear sting his eye. "For not leaving me," he softly answered.

"That's not going to happen. I think maybe someday you won't have to fall asleep on the couch," she said. "You could fall asleep next to me in bed."

"That would be nice."

"But you have to ask me to marry you first," she added. "I want to marry you in that white church and I want you to tell me you love me every day. Just don't wait too long to ask."

"I won't. I'll know when the time is right to ask. I already love you, both of you."

"We love you too. I love you."

Scarlett leaned her head on Mason's other shoulder. He kissed her head and then her lips when she looked up at him.

When their lips parted, she said, "The wide open isn't such a lonely place if you have someone to share it with."

About Jeffery Martin Botzenhart

I hate writing bios. So instead let me tell you what's on my mind. I hope you enjoyed reading

The Wide Open. Having grown up in a small town in Ohio, for years I'd been kicking around the idea of writing a story like this. There's a tranquility, an innocence, out in the wide open spaces.

Some people when first seeing this are bored by the endless nothing in sight. I think they're missing what's in front of their eyes. Every day the sky is different, filled with vivid colors or violent storms. The tall grasses bending to gentle breezes are like an expansive green ocean.

You can hear every sound and nothing at all. How could a person not find beauty in that?

Social Media

Facebook:
https://www.facebook.com/jefferymartinbot
zenhartwritingjourney/

Twitter:
https://twitter.com/@jbotzenhart

If you enjoyed this story, check out these other Solstice Publishing books by Jeffery Martin Botzenhart:

Harvest Fever
https://www.amazon.com/dp/B074JZV44F

Bullied by classmates and abused by his stepdad, seventeen year old Orrville Fletcher plans to leave his run-down home outside Birchwood Hollow, Tennessee once he turns eighteen. But one night after fighting off his stepdad, his escape from this small remote town in Appalachia is halted by an unimaginable invasion of space aliens, leading him to revelations of an unexpected truth.

Painted Desert
https://www.amazon.com/dp/B072MZY1FK

Sung with haunting vocals, a spares fragile melody strummed in the dark on a guitar can be one of many disguises for the lonely. Others, either victim of circumstance or of their own devices stay hidden behind colorful masks and pretty decorations to shield their pain. Yet these masquerades hold flaws for hearts searching to heal, revealing not desolate barren souls as any more than a painted desert, but desert angels waiting to lead the lost to the light.

Hush
https://www.amazon.com/dp/B07CSKW8Z R

Her last word before kissing him was, "Hush."

Not love at first sight, but love at first whisper. Private Gregory Sheppard's secret mission to German-occupied France has ended in tragedy. Severely injured and lacking the means to defend himself against the enemy, the help of a French woman offers him hopes of escape and a lifetime of love.

Creature of the Night
https://www.amazon.com/dp/B075ZZMGG N

Some souls were not meant to lead lives in the sun. They remain hidden within dark realms in fear of being seen and misunderstood. That is Ian's fate after suffering at the hands of a demon blinded by rage and sorrow. Yet there exists a threat in the light, spreading lies driven by fear in warning others to be weary of the unknown prowling the depths of the forest. The unyielding belief in the justification of cruelty in seeking to end that which has been branded as profane proves all consuming. When entering the forest after twilight to pronounce final judgement for those in hiding, the threshold of good versus evil is blurred by the righteous. And thus a question may be asked. Who is the true creature of the night?